ALFIE
and His Very Best Friend

For Paul and Frances with love

Other titles in the Alfie series:

Alfie Gets in First

Alfie's Feet

Alfie Gives a Hand

An Evening at Alfie's

Alfie and the Birthday Surprise

Alfie Wins a Prize

Alfie and the Big Boys

All About Alfie

Alfie's Christmas

Alfie Outdoors

Alfie Weather

Alfie's World

Annie Rose Is My

Little Sister

Rhymes for Annie Rose

The Big Alfie and Annie Rose

Storybook

The Big Alfie Out of Doors

Storybook

The Alfie Treasury

THE BODLEY HEAD

UK | USA | Canada | Ireland | Australia
India | New Zealand | South Africa
The Bodley Head is part of the Penguin Random House group of companies
whose addresses can be found at global.penguinrandomhouse.com.
www.penguin.co.uk   www.puffin.co.uk   www.ladybird.co.uk

Penguin
Random House
UK

First published 2016
001
Copyright © Shirley Hughes, 2016
The moral right of the author has been asserted

Printed in China

A CIP catalogue record for this book is available from the British Library
ISBN: 978-1-782-30061-8

All correspondence to:
The Bodley Head, Penguin Random House Children's, 80 Strand, London WC2R 0RL

MIX
Paper from
responsible sources
FSC® C018179

ALFIE

and His Very Best Friend

Shirley Hughes

THE BODLEY HEAD
LONDON

Alfie and Bernard

Alfie had a very best friend and his name was Bernard. Bernard was not always quiet and well-behaved, but Alfie's little sister, Annie Rose, liked him better than any of Alfie's other friends.

Bernard liked *her* too, because she always
laughed and laughed at all his jokes.

Bernard liked painting big pictures. Their teacher at the nursery school said that they were "very expressive".

Alfie liked painting too. His pictures were usually smaller than Bernard's. But he had once won third prize in an art competition for his picture of a motorbike man.

When Mum had her birthday, Bernard painted a big picture for her of a dragon breathing flames, and she put it up on the kitchen wall.

Alfie liked story books,
and Mum often took him
to the public library
to borrow one.

He specially liked going there at story time, when all the children sat around while the library lady read to them.

One day Mum asked Bernard if he would like to come along to story time too. Bernard was not too sure about this, because he did not like having to sit still for too long. But in the end he thought he might give it a try.

When they got there, all the children sat on the floor to listen while the library lady began a story about a bear – all except Bernard. He sat with his back to her and his eyes tightly closed.

Every time she turned the page she held up the book so that everyone could see the picture. Bernard did not look. But when she got to the exciting part of the story, he shouted, "Go on! Go on!"

When story time was over, the library lady asked Bernard if he would like to join the library so he could borrow a book and take it home. And Bernard said, "Yes, please."

The book he chose was about fast cars and aeroplanes, because these were his favourite things.

Alfie and the Scooter Race

One day when Alfie and Mum and Dad and Annie Rose were coming home from the shops, they saw a notice which said:

GRAND CARNIVAL DAY

ST STEPHEN'S PARK

JULY 25th

SIDE SHOWS

FANCY DRESS PARADE

REFRESHMENTS

SPORTS

and

UNDER 5s SCOOTER RACE

St Stephen's Park was quite near to where Alfie lived,
so of course they were all keen to go. Alfie was especially
looking forward to it because he wanted to go in for the
scooter race, and so did his friend Bernard.

Alfie thought he would not
go to the carnival in fancy
dress as it might make it
more difficult to race.

But Dad said he planned to go as a superhero.
Mum made him a cloak out of a blue curtain,
and drew a big star on a white T-shirt.

She had also trimmed a beautiful hat for Annie Rose,
decorating it with ribbons and flowers. But Annie Rose
did not like that hat at all. Every time Mum tried it on her
she threw it down. So in the end they set off without it.

When they arrived at the carnival, Alfie met up with Bernard
and they had a look at all the stalls and sideshows.
Then it was time for the under fives scooter race.

They all took their places at the starting line.

Then it was 'Ready, steady – GO!' They were off!

Alfie scooted as fast as he could. But Bernard was faster!
He was way out in front!

Just at that moment a really bad thing happened to Alfie.
His scooter skidded and he toppled off.

He hit the ground
with a big thud!

Alfie was very brave.
He tried not to cry, but
he had grazed his arm
and it was very sore. And
now he was way behind
all the others. Bernard
was still in the lead.

But when he saw what
had happened to Alfie,
Bernard stopped and
turned round.

Then he went all the way back to help him up,
and they scooted on together.

In the end the race was
won by Louise Harper.

Alfie and Bernard both came in later. But as they crossed
the finish line, everyone gave them a big cheer.

"You are a true friend,"
Dad told Bernard when
the race was over.

Dad did not win anything either. The fancy dress competition was won by Sam's dad, who was dressed as a pirate captain with a black patch over one eye.

When it was all over, Dad said: "Let's go for some ice creams, then." And that was exactly what they did.

The A B C

Alfie knew all the letters of the alphabet.
(Well, most of them.)

He had a book with all sorts of funny ways of
drawing letters which he liked to copy.

A B C D E F G H I
J K L M N O P Q R S
T U V W X Y Z

a b c d e f g h i j k l m n o
p q r s t u v w
x y z

But there was another A B C which not many people knew about, and that was the **A**lfie and **B**ernard **C**lub.

There were only two members.

Annie Rose very much
wanted to be in the A B C,
but she could not join yet
because she was too little.

The A B C met in Alfie's
secret hiding place, which
was the bush in his
back garden.

Alfie made two special membership badges out of sticky paper, one for Bernard and one for himself.

Then they decided that his old friend Flumbo could be a sort of member, so Alfie made one for him too.

And then, as Annie Rose was feeling so left out, he made another one for her.

"What do the A B C do?" asked Mum.
"Is it about good deeds?"

Alfie thought for a bit.
"Perhaps," he said. "But mostly it's
about Bernard and me being friends."